W9-COJ-884

# The Night
# the White Deer Died

## Also by Gary Paulsen

THE BOY WHO OWNED THE SCHOOL
CANYONS
THE CROSSING
DANCING CARL
DOGSONG
THE FOXMAN
HATCHET
THE ISLAND
POPCORN DAYS AND BUTTERMILK NIGHTS
SENTRIES
TILTAWHIRL JOHN
TRACKER
THE VOYAGE OF THE FROG
THE WINTER ROOM

# The Night the White Deer Died

GARY PAULSEN

Delacorte Press

Published by
Delacorte Press
Bantam Doubleday Dell Publishing Group, Inc.
666 Fifth Avenue
New York, New York 10103

This work was originally published by Thomas Nelson Inc.

The trademark Delacorte Press® is registered in the U.S. Patent and
Trademark Office.

Library of Congress Cataloging in Publication Data

Paulsen, Gary.
    The night the white deer died / by Gary Paulsen.
       p.    cm.
    Summary: A teenage girl and an old Indian are brought together
by the same haunting dream.
    ISBN 0-385-30154-5
    [1. Indians of North America—Fiction.   2. Dreams—Fiction.]
I. Title.
    PZ7.P2843Ni   1990
    [Fic]—dc20                                          89-25934
                                                          CIP
                                                          AC

Book design by B. Gold/Logo Studios

Manufactured in the United States of America

September 1990

10  9  8  7  6  5  4  3  2  1

BVG

# The Night
# the White Deer Died

# The Dream

**Janet's dream was always the same,** always ended the same way. Hung in the middle ...

In the dream it was night, with a full moon, and she was standing under a rock overhang in the mountains looking down at a small pool of water.

The water was still. Dead still. And the moon made the surface of the pond a moving piece of white, like a liquid mirror.

It was so beautiful it hurt, the pool in the moonlight, and she wanted to go down to the water's edge and move her hand in it to see if the light would move and bend.

But always it was the same. Before she could move, or just as she started to go down to the pool, a white deer emerged from the brush on the other side.

It was flat white, a young doe, and it stood in the moonlight and seemed to take light from both the moon and the pool, seemed to take beauty from both, so that Janet's breath stopped half in her lungs and half out.

Oh, she thought. Just that. Oh.

For a full second the deer stood and watched the pool and took of the light and the water and the beauty, and then, like a ballerina without music, it put forth a foot and advanced to the pool.

All in silence it happened, silence so thick and quiet there wasn't even the whistle of nothing in her ears. And she stood and watched the deer move to the pool and lower its muzzle to the water to drink, and the light on the water *did* move and bend, and the deer pulled deep of the moonlight on the pool—drew deep and long.

It was then that the Indian appeared. Not just any Indian, but *the* Indian. A brave. A warrior out of time, from before, with a shield and a small fighting headdress and no clothes except a breechclout.

The Indian came from the trees on the side of the pool and stood with one foot by the water and the other slightly back. His shield was white and strapped to his arm and covered with designs that didn't make any sense to her.

And he had a bow.

And the bow was drawn with a white arrow, everything all in white, and moonlight flashed up and down the arrow, went from the Indian's eyes down the shaft of the arrow, and out past the glistening point and moved to the deer. And as she watched, frozen, in slow motion the Indian released the shaft and the bow straightened, and the arrow moved out of the bow and across the pond; white and streaking it moved, and it was clear that the deer would never move in time, never be able to avoid the shaft.

And that's when she awakened.

With the arrow in the middle, hung in time, and moonlight over the pond, Janet always awakened, always came out of it and sat up in bed. And she was always cold and covered with perspiration when she awakened.

And without knowing why, she was always deeply, terribly afraid. . . .

**1**

**Janet Carson was the kind of fifteen-**
year-old girl who would never be called Jan. She
was Janet, with long brown hair and wide clear
eyes, and she was tall and willowy and moved with
an easy grace that would never allow abbreviation.

Other girls in her class at the all-purpose small
school of Tres Pinos, New Mexico, eyed her with
open envy—for her beauty, for her rich mother, who
did the figures in stone and who was also beautiful
and had the added mystery of being divorced,
and for the boys who flocked to Janet.

But she noticed neither the boys nor the envy
and moved instead alone in a world none of the
other girls really understood.

In the small mountain town, which was largely
Mexican, with an Indian pueblo just outside of town,
Janet was the only Anglo girl in her age group. She
had friends, but they were all older.

Her mother's friends. That's how she thought of
them. Her mother had gone back to sculpting after
the divorce in California; gone back to sculpting
and moved to the isolated town of Tres Pinos, because it was the newest and latest art colony. She'd
met "tons of talented people," who now knew Janet, and some of whom were her friends.

Sort of. Older friends were never that close, and besides, most of them drank far too much; they drank until they were mush-brained, drank until they spent all their time saying the same things over and over, and generally the things they said were of a great and lofty nature—as Janet thought of them—and were very boring.

For that reason Janet, after only the one year they'd lived in Tres Pinos, was emerging as a kind of loner, caught between a school that wasn't right for her and her mother's friends, who were not right either, and who were also too old and too locked into art.

Oh, art was all right with Janet. In fact she sculpted some in clay herself, on a small basis. But she wasn't as devoted to it as her mother's friends seemed to be, and that left her still more alone.

Not that she minded.

That's how she thought of it—that fast and tight. She was a loner, *not that she minded*—it always came in that way when she thought of herself.

I like being alone, she thought—I'm alone but I don't mind. Which of course wasn't true at all, but rather than face the fact that she didn't like being a loner, that indeed she would have loved to have friends her own age and be part of the social structure of school—rather than admit she hated the way she was living, she lied to herself.

I'm alone but I don't mind it, she thought; and she thought it so often every day since they'd moved to Tres Pinos in the mountains, where the people lived the old ways and didn't like whites, she thought it so many times every single day that in the way of such things she came to believe it herself. And because she believed it, or thought she did, she began to favor being alone.

"What a strange girl," Eloise Merkins, an older woman who wrote "precious" children's books, told

Janet's mother. "Always going off by herself that way. Do you think that's normal?"

"I don't think it's important," Janet's mother answered. She wore goggles when she worked on stone, to keep chips out of her eyes, and she raised them when she wanted to be sincere. She raised them now. "I don't think it matters that she goes off alone. It's just that time for her, the time when she changes from a girl to a woman. I used to like to be alone, and if you dig into your memory, you'll probably find that you were the same way at that age."

As a matter of fact Eloise had never been troubled by much, and had never wanted to be alone—spent most of her girlhood surrounded by chatty friends—but she wisely said nothing. Families had a way of joining together, and it was not a place for an outsider to get involved.

And whatever else they were, Janet and her mother were a family. The divorce—Janet's surgeon father had spent most of his time at work anyway and so had never been close to Janet—had brought them together with a bond that allowed no outside influence to injure either of them.

Once Janet had come into a room at a party while another artist was attacking her mother's work. The attack had been overly personal and biting and had caused Janet's mother to cry—though, to be honest, the wine at the party might have had a lot to do with the tears.

At any rate Janet, normally calm, peaceful, and serene, flew at the man like a young tigress and all but flattened him with a heavy glass bowl full of dip.

"You leave her alone," she'd screamed, surprising even herself. "You leave her alone, or I'll tear you apart!"

They were a family, Janet and her mother. And after the incident at the party nobody doubted it or challenged it.

And Janet continued to move alone through her world—alone except for the attention the boys paid her, which was flattering and obnoxious at the same time. They were so—so macho, hung up in all the stupid manhood stuff that went with being a Chicano, like the cars with moon hubcaps and muscles and fighting and knives—ahh, yes, the knives. There was so much of that, and so much toughness, that Janet shied away from dates or even being with them in school, though there were several who showed off for her regularly and followed her and made the clicking sounds to attract her attention so that she would look and they could smile and turn away. It was all a stupid game as far as Janet was concerned, complicated and ridiculous. There was one guy, named Julio—pronounced "Hulio"—she was attracted to him because his eyes were dark and he stood tall. She liked him, but there was no way she could get with him because of the macho thing.

He had let it be known around school that he thought she was all right and that maybe he wanted to date her. But he couldn't come right up and ask her because that would make him lose face, and she couldn't go up and talk to him because that would ruin her reputation as far as the school and other kids were concerned, and if her reputation was ruined, Julio wouldn't want to go out with her anymore anyway. Except for that other thing. And she wasn't about to get involved that way, so everything hung in the middle.

Like the dream.

She moved alone through her life and told herself she didn't mind, which was a lie she didn't believe, and now and then, in the nights before the dream came and kept coming, now and then she looked at her life and wondered why she bothered.

She would lie on her back in bed with the moon coming into her bedroom and making the *vigas*—the poles that held the ceiling up—look like inverted dark canyons, and she would stare and stare and wonder why she bothered.

Not to live. That she had to do. But why she bothered to lie to herself and why she bothered to live the lie until she believed it. Because in the end it didn't make any difference. Whether she lied or not didn't matter in the same way her mother thought it didn't matter if she went off alone.

Then came the dream. And with the dream came the fear that she couldn't understand—deep and cutting cold fear that was so real it almost stopped her heart when she came awake after the dream.

And though it's true that the dream stopped the wondering, the fear that left her shaking alone in the night, alone and soaked in perspiration, was a terrible thing to use to replace the wondering.

It was cold and mean and more than terrible, because it left her shaken and confused, rattled her mind until she couldn't think, and there was nothing she knew about the dream, nothing she understood.

She didn't know if she was afraid for the deer or afraid that the arrow frozen in time over the pond might miss the deer and deprive the Indian of his food, or if she was afraid *of* the Indian or afraid *for* the Indian....

She was just rattled and afraid.

And that was worse than the wondering. Worse by a mile. Worse than anything in the world.

Or at least that's what she thought then, caught in the middle. Hung like the arrow.

Of course that was before she met the fifty-three-year-old Indian named Billy Honcho, who had been a governor of the pueblo and who drank wine until he saw things not the way they used to be but the way they should have been.

That was before she met Billy, who slept in the plaza in the afternoons so that the occasional tourists could take pictures of what they thought was a typical Indian but what was really just somebody drunk and sleeping it off in the sun of the plaza.

That was before Janet met Billy and learned of wars that never were but should have been fought by braves that never existed except in dreams; before she learned that all things beautiful are sometimes ugly and that many ugly things are just waiting for beauty to come to them.

That was before Janet met Billy Honcho and fell in love.

# 2

**The first time Janet and Billy met, it** was simple enough, so simple that Janet often wondered later if it all hadn't been planned by a power she couldn't understand—almost a movement of forces.

She'd gotten up one morning at dawn after a night of fitful sleeping, a night when the dream had come and awakened her, and the peace of the early morning, when she moved out of the coolness of the adobe house into the walled courtyard, was like a cool and soothing salve on her raw nerves.

For a time she just stood in the courtyard, surrounded by the morning and by the pieces of unfinished sculpture her mother was working on; it was midsummer, and the birds were singing through the damp morning feeling, and it was all so beautiful and fresh that it was almost too rich, like eating too much sweet pastry.

She decided to take a walk. It was about half a mile from her house to the plaza in the center of town, and she set off with a long-gaited, easy stride that soon had her blood moving and muscles tingling.

All along the way there were small houses of adobe with almost ancient tilled fields around them—patchworks of green and yellow adobe. It was still too early for many people to be up, but a few roosters were cutting loose, and the sharp sound bounced down the road in front of her as though one rooster were warning the next of her coming.

In town the plaza was covered with flagstone, cut in odd shapes, and the whole square was surrounded by high cottonwoods that spread so wide they nearly met at the middle, making the plaza into almost a room, a high green room. In the center of the plaza a low building lay, actually little more than a roof at ground level, with the rest of the building buried.

This was the jail, and nobody in town knew why the original founders—over four hundred years in the past—had decided to bury the jail in the middle of the plaza. They just had, and the jail had always been there, a low flat roof, with the cells and sergeant's desk underground at the end of a slanted stairway, where it was rumored many hippies were beaten and many summer drunks who were nonlocal were roughly handled for their money. None of it had ever been proved, but the rumors persisted, and once Janet had seen a young man with long hair come out of the jail with his face all bruised, so she supposed there was some truth to it all.

But this morning when she came to the plaza she wasn't thinking of the jail so much as of the morning. Moving into the shade of the cottonwoods on the cool stone of the plaza, she sat on a concrete bench near the water fountain that was turned on in the summer and closed her eyes and let her thoughts come clean from the night and the dream, and when she opened her eyes a moment later, an old Indian was sitting next to her on the bench.

At first, for the smallest part of a second she couldn't believe he was sitting there. Not really. And she blinked once.

Then her nose caught him; the stale smell of old and tired and used wine, and she opened her eyes again. He was real.

"Oh." She said it softly, the same *oh* that came in the dream, though she didn't know it then—a tiny little acknowledgment. "Hello."

But he said nothing, looked straight ahead out across the plaza, as if she weren't there. He looked indescribably old and filthy, with a blanket wrapped around his head and upper body that had once been flannel but that now looked like greased canvas. The wrinkles in his face were caked with dirt, as were his fingernails, and his eyes had the deep red-yellow that comes from acute alcoholism, and as she studied him out of the corner of her eye, he started to lean-fall over toward her.

She stood suddenly, started to leave, half in fear and half in revulsion.

"My name is Billy." His voice was cracked and brittle, like gravel in dry leaves. "Billy Honcho. I was in jail. You got any money?"

She stopped, turned. He wasn't looking at her, was still staring straight ahead, but there was something new about him—some feeling she couldn't understand—that made her pause. Normally she would just have moved on, back into the soft morning, away from this old and drunk Indian.

"I said, 'You got any money?'" He repeated the question, still looking straight ahead. "I just got out of jail, and I need some wine."

"No ..." She answered hesitantly. She was still trying to figure out the newness of him, the feeling. "No money—I'm just out for a walk. I didn't bring any money."

"You have some at home?"

It's his shoulders, Janet thought; it's the angle of his shoulders. It's like the shoulders are fighting the rest of the body and won't admit that he's asking me for money; the shoulders are straight and level and strong. Very strong.

"What's the matter with you?" He finally turned and looked up at her, just a quick red-and-yellow-eyed look. "Ain't you ever seen a drunk Indian before?"

Caught, she nodded. "Sure. I mean . . ."

"Tscha!" He made a sound of disgust that came from his throat; almost like a cat spitting in anger, but deeper, stronger. "Little rich white girl, out seeing the poor drunk Indi'ns." He shortened the word *Indian* the way many Indians did, said it the way some tourists would have them say it. "Aren't you brave?"

"Now listen—I didn't ask to meet you out here, you know." Janet felt the anger rise and let it. "I was just out for a walk and sat down to enjoy the plaza. You're the one who came to me, remember?"

For a time there was silence. Then he smiled. "You got any money at home?" His voice was nearly a wheedle. "I mean, I'm hurtin', hurtin' bad, inside. I need some wine."

I should leave, she thought. I should leave now and be away from this dirty old man and his stink and filth. I should leave now.

But she stayed, and many times later she would wonder what it was that made her stay when everything in her wanted to leave. She stayed, and her mouth opened, and she said, "Even if you had money, there's no place to get wine. It's too early in the morning."

He smiled. He had her nailed and knew it. "Old Corky Rodriguez will open his liquor store for a dollar and will give me wine out the back door. Not for any less, but for a dollar he will open it. Do you have a dollar at home?"

I'm going crazy, she thought. I'm going completely mad. A kind of whirl went through her head, a whirl of drunks she had seen in the plaza on different occasions, drunks begging, and she had never talked to any of them, never stopped to say a word or visit or even nod, and in the whirl she saw Billy; she had seen him drunk in the plaza, begging off tourists, charging them to take pictures of the *Indi'n* with the braids and blanket, and she nodded. Instinctively, without meaning to, she nodded. "Yes. I have a dollar at home." God, she thought, I'm acting so *dumb!*

He shrugged. "Well, then, we have enough to get Corky to open the back door and give me some wine and stop this hurtin', don't we?"

Again she nodded.

"Let's go, then." He stood up and started walking, and she started following him, wondering how he could walk so fast when he looked so sick and bad.

But he shuffled, his dirty moccasins kicking up dust, and the shuffle seemed to float him over the ground as if he were on air, and she had to step fast to keep up. Through it all—following him out of the plaza and back down the road through the morning to her house, where he waited outside while she went in for a dollar and gave it to him and then watched him walk alone back up the road toward Corky's wine shop—through all of that she had no idea why she was doing it, why she gave him the dollar and talked to him or any of it. She had no reason for any of it.

And it wasn't until he was out of sight down the road that it dawned on her that he had never once asked where she lived. He'd walked ahead of her all the way, right to the door gate on the courtyard, where he'd stopped and waited for the money, and never once had he stopped to ask her where she lived.

He'd known exactly where Janet lived.

He'd known where she lived just as he'd known beforehand that she would give him the dollar. . . .

**3**

**In the middle of the summer in Tres**
Pinos there is a festival that lasts three days, or that is
supposed to last three days, though it often goes on
for a week, and it wasn't until the festival that Janet
saw Billy Honcho again.

The festival of Tres Pinos, along with being a
time of wild celebration, is also a time of maximum
tourist attraction—it's the middle of the warmest part
of the year, when something "quaint" is happening,
and they flock from miles around to join in the fun or
at least take pictures.

Local people—Indians, Chicanos, and Anglos—
all view the festival as a time to make money selling
their arts or crafts, so that with the party air there is a
definite feeling of business, and the true nature of
the festival—a kind of relief from winter's grimness—is
lost in the drive to make enough money to last the
whole year.

The end result of all this is that for most residents
of the town the festival is a time of hard work and
long hours, and Janet was no different. Her mother
was given a space on the edge of the plaza to set
up her stone figures, and Janet had to help, though
she couldn't understand her mother's drive to sell
her sculptures when there was plenty of money; the

checks came in from her father in California every month.

"It's not the money," her mother said as they hefted the heavy stone figures into the back of a borrowed pickup to take them to the plaza. "It's the recognition—artists have to be recognized for their work to mean anything."

Janet had nodded. "Still. Couldn't you work in aluminum or something? Some kind of light material?"

They'd laughed, but in truth Janet had no desire to go to the plaza. She'd told no one of the incident with Billy and had studiously avoided going downtown or near the plaza, because she knew he would be there working the tourists for drinks and money the way the others did, and she didn't want to see that, see him doing something that low. It wasn't a feeling she totally understood, because she didn't like Billy, didn't like what he'd done to her, but she still didn't want to see him doing anything degrading.

But when they'd gotten to the plaza the afternoon before the official start of the festival, the crowd had been so thick she hadn't seen any sign of Billy, and she soon forgot him in the press.

Artists and craftsmen were jammed around the plaza; all around the sides were tables and racks packed with pottery, macramé, paintings, sculpture, jewelry—everything imaginable. The huge square was like an earthy outdoor supermarket of arts and crafts, and Janet and her mother practically had to fight a wildlife artist and a girl selling macramé for room to set up their sculptures between them.

"Are you sure this is really necessary?" Janet asked, setting a fifty-pound stone nude on the flagstone and throwing one quick, angry glance at the wildlife artist, who had moved her tables into Janet's mother's space.

"It's necessary."

"Well, then . . ." And she'd been going to make some quip about hoping it was worth it, some little comment, but she stood and turned and there was Billy.

He was standing but weaving, obviously very drunk, and as dirty or dirtier than he'd been the day she'd met him alone in the plaza. Still, drunk as he was, the shoulders were straight, still fighting him.

"Hey, frien', you got any money for me?" His voice was slurred, and she realized with a start that he didn't recognize her, had no idea who she was or that he'd seen her before. "Wanna take a picture of an Indi'n?"

"Go away." Janet's mother stood up from arranging some small pieces of stonework and came between them like a mother bear protecting her cubs. "Go away, now."

"Wait, Mother." Janet put her hand on her mother's shoulder and moved her gently sideways. "His name is Billy. . . ."

"You *know* him?"

"Good picture of Indi'n," Billy cut in. "Blanket, braids, everythin'."

"Don't send him away." Janet looked up at the trees over the plaza, moved some brown hair out of her face, wondered why she was saying this, doing this. "Let him stay. Don't let him go off and be seen by the others—please."

Her mother turned to stare at her. "Have you gone out of your mind?"

"Probably." Janet nodded. "But do this favor for me, please."

Whether Janet or her mother could do anything for Billy was debatable; he was into a deep level of intoxication, drunk to the point of being unable to discern places or people, and there would have been little Janet or her mother could do either to help him or detain him.

In any case it was taken out of their hands. Before either of them could say or do anything further, Emile Gonzales, the town cop, who was all dressed fine in his best uniform for the festival, came up in back of Billy and put a hand on his shoulder.

"Come on, Billy." Emile's voice was firm, but not rough or unkind. "Quit bothering the artists—come on and sleep it off."

"Oh, he's not bothering us." Janet stepped forward to stop the arrest she thought was happening. "Not at all. He's just talking to us. . . ."

But Emile wasn't listening. He had Billy by the arm and was weaving him gently through the crowds that were building to see the festival a day before the official opening. Janet watched them until they were out of sight, going down the slanted stairway into the jail, and when she turned to help her mother, she was surprised to find that she felt truly bad, truly sorry about Billy.

It was a feeling she didn't fully understand, but it stayed with her for the remainder of that evening while they set up for the festival, and when it was night and they were finished, it still bothered her so much that she actually decided to go down into the jail and see how long they intended holding Billy.

The stairs were dank, lighted by a small yellow bulb, and they smelled of things Janet would rather not have thought about, and the entryway into the jail at the bottom of the stairs was no better. It was a small room of concrete painted an evil yellow with a gray-topped bench, and in back of the bench sat not Emile but a beefy-looking man with a scar running down the right side of his face. His color was dark except for the scar, which was almost white, and he looked at Janet up and down—slowly and insolently, but said nothing.

Janet waited a full minute, and when he still said nothing but continued to stare at her, she coughed.

"Billy," she said. "You have a man named Billy Honcho in here."

He said nothing, simply stared, waiting.

"I just wondered how long you meant to hold him." Outside, the sounds of the festival were louder now, the drinking was getting heavier—as it would continue to grow all through the celebration—and Janet wished she hadn't come down into this strange and ugly place. She turned to go; obviously she would learn nothing.

"What's he to you?"

The jailer's voice stopped her at the door, and she stood, one hand on the knob, not turning but keeping her back to him. She didn't want to see him looking at her. "A friend—he's a friend."

"Ahhh, I see. You mean old Billy found a friend somewhere? The old governor got somebody to buy his wine?"

"Governor?" She turned. "Why did you call him that?"

The jailer turned, and the light hit his scar as he moved, almost made it flash. "He used to be the governor out to the Indian pueblo—didn't you know that?"

She shook her head. "How long are you going to hold him?"

"Until the festival is over. Keep him out of the way of all them rich folks—don't want 'em seeing anything they don't like, do we?"

But Janet was gone out the door before he'd finished talking. Her mother was waiting and would wonder where she'd gone; they still had to eat a late supper and get to bed and try to get some sleep before the official start of the celebration the next morning, because after that there would be no sleep, or very little; after this first night there would be only the madness of the festival.

And besides, Janet hurried because she wanted to sleep to see if the dream came again so that she could get a chance to study the Indian with the bow. She had a hunch, a feeling that if she could see his face one more time, she would know him, but of course the dream came and ended the same way, with the arrow halfway to the deer, and she didn't really see the brave's face or get a chance to check her hunch.

**4**

**When it was all over, Janet tried to** remember the festival, come up with a feeling for it, but it came through only in disjointed pictures, images that weren't connected to each other. She couldn't remember a flow, a movement of the celebration or a reason for it all—just pictures, flashing like somebody's insane sideshow, without order or meaning.

Hot. It was hot during the days. Even with the overhanging cottonwoods the heat cooked down, and in the heat there seemed to be an endless succession of sweating, angry people, all griping about prices and all carrying very expensive cameras and wearing god-awful Bermuda shorts and colored shirts and blouses and tank tops, and everybody had to *touch* everything, grab and clutch and scream and pull and . . .

It was incredible. Janet and her mother had never seen a festival before, but Janet swore that if she lived through this one, recognition or not, she'd never do another.

There was the man from Texas who came with a truck, a huge rented truck, and bought paintings he thought would be good investments. He did not buy them for their art or looks—he didn't even really look at them—but because he might make money on them. He just bought them and loaded them into the truck, and when the truck was full, he pulled away, and everybody watched him drive through the crowded streets until he was out of sight.

There was the little old lady in the wildly striped pantsuit who decided she wanted a stone head carved by Janet's mother, only she didn't want to pay for it. Janet had been talking to an unlistening couple from Pasadena, the kind who ask questions but don't wait for an answer before the next question, and when she turned, the little old lady was struggling to walk off with the head.

Since the sculpted stone head weighed just over seventy-five pounds, it was a losing battle; but the old lady tried and was downright indignant when Janet caught up with her and took the head back where it had been.

There were people everywhere, people and money and more people and more money. Janet couldn't believe it, didn't in a way *want* to believe it.

"It's as though a huge pen with all the poor-taste people in the world had been opened, and they've all come to the festival," Janet said the second night while they were staggering into the house to eat a cold snack and drop into their beds. "From these people you want recognition?"

"I'll discuss artistic philosophies later." Her mother sighed. "Right now I'm for bed, and I don't even *care* if I sell anything."

But she did sell—they came to buy, and along with all the other artists and craftspeople at the festival, Janet's mother sold everything she'd brought, could have sold more, could have sold anything.

"I'm going to try a brick," Janet said at one

point. "Find me a brick, and I'll label it art, and we'll see if we can get ten dollars for it. . . ."

It was a joke, but it probably would have worked. One girl down the way four booths was selling decorative wood, driftwood from the gullies out of town, and when she ran out, she sent a friend out with a pickup to one of the gullies to get a load of wood—wood that most of the locals burned as firewood—which she sold right out of the truck for four and five dollars a small piece, and the crowds were crushing each other to get to the truck.

It was madness. An insane rush of pushing people wanting to buy, to see art and the artists. Heat and crowds . . . screaming and shoving . . . splashes of color . . . cameras clicking . . . dust. . . . And just when it seemed to Janet that she could stand no more, that she was going to crack, just then she turned, and there was Julio.

His eyes were arrogant, black and distant, and he stood tall in elevated shoes, and he startled her until she looked down and saw that he was holding out a quart jar full of ice and brown liquid.

"Iced tea." He made it a statement, simple and flat, but he kept his eyes averted, looking over her head because of the macho thing and because they did not truly know each other yet. "It is for you."

Janet looked at the jar. The sides glistened with condensed moisture and cold droplets running down, and she thought she'd never seen anything so wonderful as that tea. She took it and swallowed a long draft, found that it had just a touch of sugar, and handed it to her mother, who also took a long swallow.

"Thanks, Julio," Janet said, rubbing the cool glass across her forehead. "That's great—just perfect."

But he was gone before she'd finished the sentence, vanished in the crowds before anybody saw him talking to her—part of the festival, part of the wild week of the midsummer celebration that had started long ago—nobody knew when and for what reason originally.

The wild summer festival of Tres Pinos—Janet had heard about it but never seen it before. When it was over, after winding down like a tired maniac, still insane but too exhausted to do anything about it, when it was all finished, there were four days and nights gone out of her life. All her mother's art was sold and gone, and Janet looked at the empty rubble of the plaza and couldn't believe that it all had happened. Not really.

It was the end of the fourth day, just getting dark, soft dusk-dark. Most of the artists were gone, and Janet and her mother stood virtually alone—for the first time in four days—except for a few people moving to parties that always seemed to go hand in hand with the festival.

"I feel . . . feel wasted." Janet flopped her arms and sighed. "Used . . ."

"I know what you mean." Her mother took a deep breath, let it out, brushed some hair out of her eyes, and looked down at her tank top and jeans. A spot had appeared on the right side of the tank top, a dark spot so obscure that at first she didn't see it, and when she did, she wiped at it gingerly—as though not certain it was really there. "I didn't know it was going to be this wild—had no idea. Nobody told me."

Her voice was half apologetic, and she looked at Janet beseechingly. Janet had never felt so close to her mother; right then, at that instant, she loved her more than anything on earth. But it was more than that. She viewed her as a close friend as well, and without really thinking she went over to her mother and put her arms around her. It was a rare instant of genuine closeness, an almost beautiful moment, and when they parted, it was with reluctance.

"Well." Janet's mother looked around and shrugged. "It's over, that's something."

"But what a mess." Janet gestured around them. The plaza was covered with trash, paper, food and drink containers, junk. "Who gets to clean this up?"

As though on cue, she heard a sound to her rear and turned to see the jailer coming up the stairway from the jail. In back of him were four inmates, all arrested for being drunk.

"Clean it," the jailer told them. "When you're done, you can go, but make sure it's clean, or I'll have you back in the hotel."

He turned and went back down into the jail, a troll returning to his underworld dwelling, and the four released drunks began picking up papers and putting them in the trash containers at the corners of the plaza.

One of the four men was Billy, looking dirty but surprisingly spry and alert. Janet started to call to him but then realized that it would only embarrass him. Instead she moved with her mother away from the plaza, across the street to the small café where they'd eaten dinner every evening.

But they got a booth by the window, where LA CANTINA ... FINE MEXICAN FOOD was lettered, and after ordering burritos and chili and milk, Janet looked out the window through the lettering and watched Billy picking up trash while they waited for their food, and she thought how degrading it was that a man who used to be governor would have to do that, clean up after other people. When the chili came, she was still thinking about it, wondering if that might be called part of the festival, and she worried over it so much that she had three bites of chili down before she realized it was the hot version and that her mouth was on fire.

Then of course she gulped her milk, had to drink three glasses before the fire was out and she could breathe again. And when she once more looked out through the lettering, Billy was gone from the plaza.

5

**In the summer before fall but after**
the festival the town of Tres Pinos goes into a quiet
period, almost like an animal licking its wounds or
resting after a long fight, and it was during this time
that Janet again saw Billy Honcho.

Julio had been around some, still not too openly,
but he was getting braver. Twice he had walked off
to the side of Janet when she went into town, far
enough off so anybody seeing them couldn't be
sure they were together but close enough to call to
her and tell her that he was a good fighter and that
if she ever had any trouble to let him know and he'd
fix it.

Once he'd spent most of the day by the gate
on the courtyard of the house, just standing and
flipping rocks, and he was so unsubtle that Janet's
mother asked about him.

"He's just a friend," Janet answered. "Well, sort
of, I guess."

"Classic form—he'd be fun to sculpt. Tall, mus-
cular, willowy. Why not invite him in to model?"

"He won't come."

"Try."

So Janet had gone out to ask Julio if he wanted
to model for her mother while she sculpted, and

he'd made a sound of scorn. "I should allow myself to be used in this way?"

"Sure." Janet had shrugged. "It isn't bad or anything—just art. Because you've got a classic form."

That caught him, and she could tell he felt flattered, but he was still too shy and thought it was too degrading—perhaps—for him to do. Yet. So he moved off down the dusty street, and it was while watching him go that time, watching his arrogance as he walked, that Janet saw Billy.

He was farther down the street, walking bent over with a tight little shuffle, and when she saw him, he happened to be looking in her direction, and she waved. It was natural, a quick wave, and she was surprised when he came toward her.

She waited, squinting in the sun, leaning against the gate, and when he got close, she could tell that he was sober—dirty, but sober.

"Hi." Janet kept her voice even, but she found with a shock that her heartbeat was speeding up and that she had a strange shy feeling.

"The girl with the dollar," Billy said when he stopped at the gate. "The girl with the dollar for the wine."

Janet nodded but said nothing; she was still trying to analyze the feelings she had. The sun was hot, but not hot enough for the perspiration that suddenly came onto her forehead.

It was his eyes; she was certain of it. They weren't red, didn't look yellow or drunk or stupid. Instead they were steady and looked inside her and saw things that she wasn't sure she wanted him to see. Or at least that's how she felt, standing in the sun, sweating as he gazed at her.

"I saw you in the park." He had a way of talking in clipped words so that there could never be an argument about anything he said, and he gestured the way many Indians did when they talked, his arms and hands flowing with the words, making things almost visible so that the words seemed to come to life. "I saw you in the plaza when you saw me but didn't call and went into the eating place. You watched me through the window while you ate."

She started. "I didn't think you saw me. I mean ..."

"That night I got some wine from Corky, and me and two other fellas we sat down by a little water, and we got drunk and sang, all down by the creek between town and the pueblo." His eyes perked, took on a half-sideways, wizened look. "Maybe so if you'd talked to me in the park, I wouldn't have gone down by the creek and gotten drunk on the cheap wine with the fellas."

"Oh, no." Janet shook her head. "I'm not going for that. It's not my fault you got wine and got drunk—not at all."

He smiled. Suddenly a quick jerk of his lips—out and back. "Come. Let's walk."

Before she could answer, he started off down the road, not toward town but away, and without knowing for certain why she was doing it, Janet opened the gate on the courtyard and followed him. It was hot now, very hot, and his step-shuffle kicked up small puffs of dust with each step, and she caught herself staring down at them as she followed him.

He walked that way for nearly a quarter of a mile without speaking to her, and Janet was on the edge of getting angry when he stopped and turned so fast she nearly bumped into him.

"You ever been to the pueblo?" He pointed with a graceful wave on down the road where the pueblo lay, about two miles out of town. "You ever see where Indi'n live?"

She shook her head. "Well, once. I almost forgot. When we first came to Tres Pinos, Mother and I drove out there to take some pictures, but there was some kind of dance or celebration going on and we couldn't get in because ... because we're white. Anglo."

"No." He shook his head. "Not because you're Anglo."

"Yes ..."

"No! It was because you're *not* Indi'n that you couldn't come in. There's a big difference."

He turned and shuffled off again in the direction of the Indian town, and Janet followed, exasperated. He had the most maddening way of stopping in what seemed like the middle of a discussion, stopping when he'd finished talking and not waiting to see what she had to say about it.

"You're pretty," he said suddenly over his shoulder without stopping or turning. "You know that?"

"I ... I never really thought about it before."

"That's a lie."

"Well—what did you expect me to say? That's kind of a strange thing to say, isn't it? Right out of the blue like that."

"Don't lie. You know you're pretty, say it. You never have to lie."

"All right! I'm pretty—I guess. There, are you satisfied?"

"Not for me," he said, still over his shoulder while he walked. "For you. You got pretty hair. Long, straight."

When he didn't say anything further, Janet thought he expected an answer, and she fairly yelled at him.

"I *know* I've got pretty hair. I comb it every morning. Yes, it's pretty hair."

"Pretty chin, too."

"I *know* I've got a pretty chin. . . ."

"No. Too square. Don't lie. Think. Your chin isn't pretty, just your hair."

She wasn't sure, but she thought she might have heard a faint chuckle before he resumed silence and the quick little steps that took them on out of Tres Pinos on a narrow road lined with tall cotton-woods dropping fluff and coolness on them as they moved. When it seemed to Janet that she couldn't go much farther, he stopped.

"See? Indi'n house, where I live."

Janet pulled up and looked, and sure enough, they were at the entrance of the pueblo. The two miles had taken practically no time to cover, and she wasn't even breathing hard—though she was perspiring heavily.

The pueblo was beautiful, ancient and beautiful sitting in the hot sun. It was made all of adobe con-struction, and the color was a subtle beige-red earth tone that was so natural and fine that it nearly took Janet's breath away to see it. It was a series of small apartments, stacked three high, arranged in a **U**-shape with a wall across the open end of the **U**, all of adobe bricks and hand-plastered with adobe mud so that it almost looked sculpted, with no straight lines but gentle curves on every corner and around every door and window. In the courtyard formed by the closed-in **U** there were several large domed objects made of adobe with small openings in the side. These, she knew, were earthen ovens for baking bread—once she'd eaten some of the bread with her mother at a sale the Indian women had in town—but they looked more like giant beehives made of rich earth.

"It's a good place." Billy's voice was straight and level, smooth and low, and she turned and saw that he was smiling as he looked at the pueblo. "It's a good place."

She nodded. "It's beautiful—old and beautiful." She had read once that pueblos were the oldest continually lived-in structures in North America; some of them had been inhabited for thirteen hundred consecutive years—Indians living all those years in the same buildings, adding apartments as needed wherever the population expanded past the normal number of a thousand or so.

"It's a fine place to live," she agreed. "A great place ..."

He shrugged suddenly, and she could sense the mood change in him, as though he'd been caught doing something private and didn't want her to see it.

"You got a dollar?" He looked at her. "I'm hurtin' for some wine."

This time she shook her head. "No. No dollar. Not even at home."

"So. Maybe so you go home to your home, and I'll go into Indi'n home if you don't got a dollar." His voice had reverted to the chopped sound. "Maybe so you better leave now."

And he turned and went into the pueblo and left her standing, not really believing that he'd done it to her, not wanting to believe it, until it was obvious that he wasn't coming back out of the beautiful earthen structure and that he'd really just left her standing alone two miles out of Tres Pinos on a dirt road and wasn't going to invite her into the pueblo.

Then she swore once, viciously, using a word she'd heard Julio use one night when he'd screamed at the police as they drove by, and then she began the long walk back to her house and a cool bath to slow her anger.

**6**

**It was the next morning, early, and**
Janet was just coming out of sleep with that warm,
loose feeling. She hadn't had the dream and was
lazily wondering how to spend the day, because it
was only one more week until school started and
she didn't want to waste the week.

There was sun outside, and warm morning smells
in the house, and she was wrapping her mind around
the idea of breakfast when her mother knocked
gently and came into her room.

She was wearing her old tie-around housecoat
and had one hand behind her back. She sat on the
foot of the bed and looked at Janet.

"Is there some part of your life you'd like to tell
me about, Janet?" Her voice was light, but her eyes
were serious. "Something you think I might want to
know?"

Janet sat up, stretched, yawned. "No. I can't think
of anything. Why?"

"Well, no real reason. I mean I don't want you
to think I'm prying. But when I went out for the goat
milk"— they had fresh goat milk delivered every
morning—"I found this next to our gate." She brought
her hand from behind her back and placed an
object on the bed next to Janet.

Out of the corner of her eye Janet caught the movement of hair and grayness, and she yelped and jumped. "What's that?"

Her mother laughed. "Don't worry, it's not alive. It's a kachina. . . ." She picked it off the bed where it had dropped and handed it to her daughter.

"A kachina?" Janet took the object and found it to be a doll, made of wood and clay with what looked like real black hair but was probably horse-hair. It was a figure of an Indian dancing, crude but powerfully done, dressed in small bits of cloth and wearing real tiny leather moccasins. "A kachina?"

Her mother nodded. "A doll used in instructing Indian children in the ways of the god messengers. I read up on them before we moved to Tres Pinos. This is a rain messenger, or a doll showing how a man would costume himself to dance as a rain messenger to the gods asking for water for the corn crop."

"But . . ."

"People used to think the dolls were the god messengers, but they're just tiny figures to teach the Indian children." Her mother recited as though out of a textbook. "At last count there were over three hundred different kachinas, with a doll for each one, each carrying a different message to the gods."

"But why is there one on *our* gate?" Janet finally got through.

"Exactly. I was going to ask you that question."

"Me? But I can't think of anybody who would . . ." She let it fall off when she remembered Billy's leaving her at the gate of the pueblo. "Unless it's Billy—maybe he left it."

"Billy? Who's Billy—oh, that old drunken Indian?"

"Mother."

"Well. How about old alcoholic Indian—do you like that better?" Her eyebrows lifted. "And while we're discussing it, you might tell me how it is that you've gotten involved with him?"

"It's nothing. There's just something about him, something about his shoulders or eyes or something. I don't really know." Janet studied the kachina, turned it over in her hands. The carving had been colored with earthen dyes and had the same naturally rich look with which the pueblo had shone when she'd seen it in the hot light with Billy before he'd left her at the gate.

On the leather breechclout there were painted a series of blue and white fluffy things she took to be clouds, and lightning bolts cut through the clouds.

"Well, it's a nice gift, to be sure." Her mother held her hand out and took it and restudied it. "It really is." She left Janet's room and put the small figure on the dresser on the way out. "Odd thing to find on the gate when you go out for goat milk. . . ."

Janet hurried to finish dressing. When she'd climbed into jeans and a tank top and tennis shoes, she stopped for a quick glass of juice and a piece of toast and then went outside, where the sun was already heating the dust in the road. But look as she might, she couldn't see Billy anywhere in the vicinity.

She hadn't really expected to find him, wasn't truly sure Billy had left the kachina—it might even have been Julio. He'd come to the gate, was hanging around more; maybe he'd left the doll for her. It would be strange, but not impossible.

Still, there was something about it all that made her think of Billy, and when she heard the *chink-chink* of her mother starting to sculpt stone, she decided to find Billy and tell him thanks for the doll. Her mother would be at it all day anyway—she was getting more and more into her work and away from everything else. Not that it was wrong, Janet thought, going through the gate and into the street, but it was oddly like living alone when you were with somebody like that. Twice she'd gone into the low room her mother used for a studio and talked to her while she was sculpting and was fairly certain her mother hadn't heard a word—she'd just nodded, worked and nodded and ignored her. But in a nice way. And she wasn't drinking or going to parties so much anymore either; nor was she having parties at home or entertaining the phony artists and writers as much as she did when they first came to Tres Pinos. For that Janet was thankful.

She moved in the direction of town, not sure where to look but feeling it was the right way to go, and thought of her mother while she walked. A dog followed her, circled shyly when she turned and called to it, stayed an acceptable street distance from her but kept following, and Janet wondered if it was a stray and if she should keep it.

She'd worried right after the divorce. Her mother had become involved more with the phony side of living than the real; the "artists" she'd had to the house were talkers and not doers, and Janet had worried that her mother would get caught in the trap, just being social and not doing anything with her talent, not doing what she really wanted to do.

God, she thought, remembering when they'd first moved to the small mountain desert town, and all the so-called artists had started showing up for free meals and drinks—always drinks. Always. They were so . . . just *so*.

Like parasites of some kind they were, talking heavy art and getting drunk, and nobody was working or doing anything but eating and drinking and playing around. It was sickening to Janet, sickening and like a stupid game of some sort, with idiotic rules that only worked in the art colony and didn't matter to the outside world.

And for a time, perhaps because she was reacting to the divorce, Janet's mother had seemed to be falling into the trap like the rest of them. She seemed to be talking "artsy" in gushes and staying drunk and playing around and going to parties, to which she dragged Janet along and where Janet would have to stand and listen to half-sloshed artsy painters talk about her innocent beauty and charm. . . .

It could gag flies, she thought, turning once more to see if the dog would come to be petted. It came closer, but still maintained a safe distance, and Janet continued on into town.

But her mother had snapped out of it, had stayed out of the trap. One day she'd started sculpting, and when the phonies had come around, she'd just told them she was working and would call them when she was finished, and that naturally angered them so much they quit coming around.

Since then everything had been fine, at least between Janet and her mother.

She stopped again. She was at the edge of the downtown section of Tres Pinos and wasn't sure where to look for Billy.

Either in the plaza or at the back door of Corky's liquor store, she thought, and then felt bad because it was an unkind thing to think. It was only midmorning and still too early for Billy to be drunk. But even so, knowing that, she moved in the direction of Corky's liquor store, and when she got there and nobody was at the front, she went to the back, and there was Billy, sitting on the ground by the back door with a bottle in a paper sack. And knowing it was wrong, *knowing* with every fiber in her body that it was wrong, she went over and sat down beside him in the dirt and leaned against the wall.

**7**

**Billy said nothing. Indeed for the long-**
est time she wasn't sure he even knew she was
there. The two of them sat in the sun leaning against
the warm adobe, and a fly moved around them,
with a light buzzing as it moved to the back door of
the liquor store and returned over them, and the
dog that had been following Janet now came up
and nuzzled her fingers, which she had draped
over one of her knees.

"You have a dog." Billy's voice was only slightly
slurred. "I didn't know you had a dog."

"No. It just followed me." Janet pet the dog on
the side of its muzzle; it was soft and damp. Pleas-
ant. "It's just an old dog. . . ."

"Why are you here?" The sack rose, and she
heard the gurgle of wine; one, two, and then three
swallows. Then the sack lowered. "Why did you come
and find me and sit next to me here in the back of
Corky's? You better leave. Maybe you better leave
now before the others come to sit and drink in the
sun."

He stopped, and Janet shrugged. "I came to
thank you for the kachina. I found ... I mean my
mother found it this morning by the gate when she

went out for milk. I just wanted to thank you for leaving it."

"How do you know it was me?" He snorted. "It could have been anybody. . . ."

"But it was you, wasn't it?"

He nodded. "Yes. But you could not know that—it was a lucky guess."

"And you left it because you felt sorry about leaving me at the gate of the pueblo yesterday."

She knew she shouldn't have said it the moment it slipped out; she could feel him tighten against the wall.

He fell back into silence, took another swallow of wine, and she sensed that she'd hit his pride somehow. She relaxed back against the wall, put her hand on the dog's head, closed her eyes, and copied his silence for three or four minutes. Then she coughed lightly. "It was a good present, a good kachina."

For a time he said nothing, then he let out a bitter little laugh that seemed to cut through the heat. "It was nothing—just a toy. I won it in a poker game from a Hopi when we were both drunk, and it's only a doll for tourists."

"Still." She made a vow not to let him anger her. "Still, it is a nice thing to give me, and I thank you for it."

"Someday I will take it back, and then I will be an Indi'n giver." He laughed, and this time there was scorn in it, scorn, and more of the wine was beginning to show through.

"Don't—don't do that." She reached out but stopped before her hand touched him; looked over at him, saw that his eyes were closed and that his head was starting to lean forward. "Don't make stupid jokes like that or put yourself down."

"Ahh, what do you know?" He coughed, took another swallow of wine, and now the bottle was empty, and he threw it into some low bushes off to the side of the liquor store. It landed with a crash of broken glass on all the other broken bottles in the bush, and he opened one eye to stare at her. "You got a dollar? I'm really hurtin' for some wine."

She shook her head. "Why don't you come home with me, and I'll cook something and you can drink some coffee?"

"Tscha! Why don't *you* come home with *me,* and we'll drink some wine, and I'll tell you all about what it's like ... what it's like ... what it's like...."

He wound down like a tired phonograph, wound down and sat staring at the dirt between his legs. She noticed for the first time that his blanket was clean and new and that his braids were freshly done where they hung down the sides of his face and that he was wearing clean jeans and a new shirt. He was all fresh and new, and it hurt her to realize that he'd dressed new and cleaned up to see her that morning when he came with the kachina and then changed his mind and not waited but left the doll.

"Hey-*uh,* hi-*uh,* hopa-*hi,* hey-*uh."* He sang under his breath, an almost guttural chant. She couldn't understand the words but the sound was of the earth and pretty in a blunt way, and she made up her mind that she was going to get him home and fed and sobered whether he wanted to or not and whether he liked her or not.

"Come on." She stood up and reached down for his hand and pulled him—she was shocked to feel how light he really was—to his feet. "Come on, let's walk."

By this time the wine had genuinely come to the bottom, and he was thoroughly, almost professionally drunk; he could walk, but only just, and he made no objection at all to any of her demands.

He stood when she pulled, walked in the direction she tugged—though *stumbled* might be a better word than *walked*—and indeed it seemed to Janet that he didn't really know he was up and moving, or that she was there beside him.

"Hey-*uh,* hi-*uh* . . ." As they moved away from the liquor store—Billy, Janet, and the dog—he burst once more into singing, and after they'd gone a hundred yards down the dusty street, he stopped and shook her hand away and sang a complete song with his hands raised to the heavens while she stood off to the side looking at him, thinking he looked like some picture she might have seen of an Indian singing to his gods before a hunt. And when he was done singing, she took his arm once again and led him down the street.

"What was that song?" she asked, after they'd gone another hundred yards. And when he didn't answer, she repeated the question, but he wouldn't, or couldn't, answer and chose instead to reach with his free hand up and touch her hair.

"Pretty hair." His voice was a slur. "You have pretty hair—wrong color, but pretty."

"Thank you." She pulled his hand down and led him once more down the street, and in this manner she finally got him to her house, where he came inside easily enough. She put him in a kitchen chair while she took a bowl of leftovers back out to the dog, which had *not* wanted to come into the house.

When Janet returned, she found her mother standing in the entryway of the kitchen. She'd been in the studio when Billy and Janet came in, and she now turned to Janet.

"Out." Her voice was brittle. "I mean out. Period."

"Mother."

"No."

"Mother. He brought the kachina this morning, and he *needs* help. Please."

Janet's mother studied the figure of Billy slumped on the kitchen table. "He needs help, I'll give you that."

"Well."

"I'd rather not, Janet."

"Just some food and coffee."

"Well—all right. Just a meal. Then out, period."

"Also, Mother . . ." Janet tried to make her voice soft.

"What?"

"Outside, in the courtyard. There's a dog, just a small dog, and it followed me uptown to get Billy and back, and I fed it."

"And to think it was luck that brought me a daughter. I could have had a son." But she smiled, if tightly, and Janet knew she'd won and turned to the task of cooking a meal for Billy. She was well into scrambling eggs and brewing fresh coffee when Billy sat up suddenly and began singing again, the same song he'd stopped to sing in the road with his arms raised. And when he finished this time, he flopped his head on his arms on the kitchen table and was out, gone and under, and Janet was faced with the unpleasant prospect of either force-feeding an unconscious man or eating half a dozen scrambled eggs herself.

Then she remembered the new dog, which she still hadn't named, and carried the eggs and bacon outside, and the dog ate them ravenously.

After that Janet went back into the kitchen, where Billy was still passed out, and sat across the table and waited, with the coffee on the stove and hot, waited for Billy to sleep it off so that she could feed him and talk to him some more. And it was while she was waiting that she began to wonder if

Billy had ever shot a deer by a pond with a bow and arrow, and it wasn't too long after that, with Billy mushed head-down on the table, that she caught herself wondering what Billy had looked like when he was a young brave.

And that seemed harmless enough, that thinking, but it quickened her, and that she couldn't understand and wasn't sure she wanted to understand, sitting in her kitchen with an old drunk who had passed out on her kitchen table.

# 8

*Come to us,*
*With your black skirts.*
*Come to us,*
*Soaring.*
*Come to us with your black skirts soaring.*


**Billy sang the words in English, though** his voice still had the wild singsong lilt that made it sound as if coming from the earth, from all the earth places.

When he'd finished the song, he took another drink of coffee and sat straight in the chair, looking dead ahead as the coffee went down and did its magic work.

He'd been passed out for nearly two hours— two hours while Janet sat and read and the sound of her mother sculpting rock hovered continually in the background; and it did not seem strange to Janet to be sitting reading a book waiting for an Indian to regain consciousness on her kitchen table.

She'd been in the kitchen when he came out of it. And it had happened just that fast; suddenly he raised his head, straight and level, and coughed a bit and blinked.

"How long was I out?" He'd asked the question without looking at her, without acknowledging her presence really.

"Two hours. You were ... asleep for two hours. Maybe a little more."

Then he'd suddenly burst into song, or rambling poetry, or whatever it was—it was somehow more than music, all about the clouds and black skirts and soaring. And he'd done it in English so that she could understand, and when he'd finished singing and put the empty cup down, she refilled it and put the pot back on the stove and sat down at the table.

"That was beautiful—a beautiful song. What is it all about?"

"Rain." He said it short, nearly gruff. "It's about rain—an old Navajo chant for rain to make the corn grow so they don't have to use irrigation. It's all about rain, water. Maybe so you got some sugar? This coffee would be better with sugar."

She went to the cupboard and got sugar and made a face when he put four spoonfuls in the small cup and drank it hot and sticky-sweet, smacking his lips.

"I sing the song because it has much beauty in it and makes me feel better when I don't feel so good. Like now." He looked at her out of the corner of his eye. "You got a dollar for Corky? I'm really hurtin' for some wine."

She shook her head. "No. No more dollars for wine."

"What was all that singing?" Janet's mother suddenly appeared at the kitchen doorway. "Oh, it was you. You're up."

Strangely Billy stood up when he saw her. "Yes. I'll be out of here in a minute. . . ."

"You don't have to do that." She tossed a look to Janet. "Not really—I'd have kicked you out before if I objected to having you around."

"Well, I don't want to be in the way. Maybe so you got a dollar for some wine, and I'll be getting out of your way."

"No."

"Billy!" Janet cut in. "I said no more money for wine...."

"I'm going back to work. Remember our agreement, Janet." Her mother left the room, and Billy sat once more at the table and finished the coffee and then he stood, abruptly, and started for the door.

"Where are you going?" Janet followed him.

"Out.

"Yes, but out where? I mean why are you leaving so fast?" They were outside now, and he went through the gate without looking back, and she followed still, not sure why, until they got into the middle of the street, and there he stopped and turned on her so that she practically stumbled into him.

"Why do you do this?"

His voice remained level, but she could detect a slight plaintive note in it, and it threw her so that for a moment she couldn't answer, and when she did come up with something, it wasn't much.

"I don't know," she said, and it was only half truth, but it was all she wanted to tell him.

"You follow me, and I am an old man, and you won't give me money for wine, and you keep trying to make me eat and drink coffee and be good when I don't want those things. Why do you do this?"

"I ..." She shrugged. "It just happened, that's all."

"You came this morning and sat beside me at the back door of Corky's liquor store and wouldn't let me get happy drunk. You want me sober. Why is this? What does it mean to you if I am drunk or I am sober?"

There was nothing of anger in his voice, only the question, and she wondered if she should tell him about the dream, about all of it, but knew that she couldn't. Not now, anyway.

"Once I had a wife named Easter," he said, quickly smiling. "She was not too much but all right, all right, and stayed with me until she died of the disease that eats, and she was this way, always this way. Maybe so you're doing the same thing as my wife Easter, and that's not so good because you aren't my wife."

"No." She shook her head. "No, it's not like that...."

"Maybe so you're just one of those little white girls that likes to meddle with Indians and make them do things or not do things because it makes you feel big?"

"No, Billy ..."

"Then why do you do this?"

"It's ... oh, I don't know. I just have to do it. Ever since that first morning when I was sitting on the park bench in the plaza and you got out of jail and came and sat next to me ... and then this morning, when you came by with the kachina." She was gushing but couldn't stop, didn't want to stop. "I just knew it was you, and that you'd be by the gate, and when you weren't, I had to come looking for you, and if you really want a reason, I suppose it's because I love you...."

It was out before she could stop it, out and across the dirt into the heat of the midday before she could control it.

"Sort of. You know ..." She added it lamely, tacked it on knowing it wouldn't work, wouldn't help. "The way people love all people, you know. That way."

For a moment they stood in silence, and she looked down at her feet and saw that there was dust on the tops of her shoes, and she thought, how strange that there should be dust on *top* of my shoes. And for a little time that became the most important thing in her life, that dust, and she concentrated on it with all her might but knew she was going to have to look up sooner or later.

And when she finally did look up, his eyes were on her evenly, with a look she couldn't comprehend, had never seen before; it was a combination of pain and peace, that look, a kind of mixture of all the good and all the bad in the world, all evening out at the same time.

She wanted to say more, wanted to make it all right, but knew that anything she said would ruin something that was already damaged, so she kept her mouth shut, and he turned after a minute or a year or a life and walked off in the direction of the pueblo. She knew that she couldn't follow, not this time, so she just stood and watched him move with that curious step-shuffle that made him look as if he were floating effortlessly over the ground.

And she wanted to call after him, wanted to say "Billy" because she knew now—knew that he was the brave in the dream because of the look she'd seen in his eyes, but she didn't call; though her lips formed the word, no sound came, and she just watched until he was out of sight in the dust and heat.

# 9

**For a week she neither saw nor heard** Billy, and when ten days had passed with no contact and school had started in the ·new building north of town, up against the rugged mountains, there was too much in her life for her to think an awful lot about Billy.

School was as strange as before, almost bizarre. She was the only Anglo, except for one grade-school child who belonged to one of the teachers, and many of the other kids shunned her for that reason. But about an equal number of them seemed attracted to her for the same reason, and getting settled into classes and school life again amounted to a confused muddle of trying to evaluate whether a new acquaintance was going to be a friend or an enemy.

And always there was Julio, hovering in the background, walking behind her on the way home, making the little sounds, giving her candy and once some wrist jewelry, which he would hand her and move away before somebody saw them together—always there was Julio.

In some ways she liked having Julio interested in her. He was a powerful figure in school and kept other boys from hassling her, kept her life relatively smooth when it could have been otherwise. But no other boy would talk to her with Julio in the vicinity, out of fear and respect, and when school had been going for nearly two weeks and she'd begun to feel a bit like a very exclusive leper, Janet had stopped Julio on the way home one afternoon and braced him.

"Look. You have to give me a break." She'd caught him completely off guard as he was rounding a corner to follow her.

"What do you mean?" Immediately he took what Janet called The Stance—tall, half-angled away from her, brooding, arrogant, but poised and ready. "What kind of break?"

"I'm not your private girl or something," she'd said, and was surprised to feel the anger come into her voice. She wasn't really angry at him, but there it was—rising hotly to the surface. "You've got me locked into something I don't want to be into."

For a full minute he looked at her in offended silence. Then he turned and walked off, leaving her standing, and she wasn't certain if he'd understood or not.

At any rate it made little difference, because by the time another week had gone by, it was quite evident that whether Julio allowed her freedom or not, the other boys wouldn't dare ask her on a date. Julio quit following her, quit making the sounds at her to get her attention so that she could look at him and be ignored, but it made no real change except that now *nobody* was around her.

Except the girls, of course, but it was difficult for her to be friendly with them to any great depth because their lives were so vastly different from hers.

Not bad, not good, the way her life was not bad, not good to them—just different. And the difference was so profound that she knew she could never change enough to become true friends with any of them, at least not for years.

And her mother was working very hard, too, now that the hot summer was over. The crisp nights and soft days of fall, with splashes of gold in the aspens as they dropped their leaves and the almost unbelievable beauty of high desert and low mountains as they turned their faces to winter had come into their lives so subtly that Janet couldn't really remember ever having lived anywhere else. Nor wanting to—she was due to visit her father in California for Christmas, and as much as she loved her father, she was wondering if she could get out of it.

There was too much beauty here to leave, and even being basically alone—when her mother was deep into sculpting, nothing else existed—Janet was not unhappy.

The dog followed her always, though she still hadn't named him, and in a strange way the small animal filled that part of her life that would normally have been lonely or sad.

Even the dream had ceased coming, and she had to force herself to remember when it had last come or just how it went; some of the images in the dream, the doe and the pond, were blurred in her memory, and now and then she smiled when she remembered the significance she'd given the dream.

It was all so silly, she thought now, so little-girlish and silly. The whole thing, the dream and the way it had scared her for no reason and the way she would wake up drenched with perspiration, and the way the dream took her mind, made her part of it all, was all so ridiculous that she now wondered sometimes if perhaps she hadn't been a little off, a little crazy.

Maybe she was having trouble changing from a girl to a woman, she thought one cool evening halfway through the month of November, when there was a taste of winter in the air—a tease—and she sat alone in the kitchen while the *chink-chink* of her mother's hammer and chisel came from the studio room. But then she smiled and thought that all of *that* was silly, too, just like her strange infatuation with Billy had been, or the hot anger that came when she talked to Julio, or the fact that she was sitting now alone in her kitchen even *thinking* about all the silly things that had been bothering her. She was on top of things right then; right at that moment, she would think later, she was in complete control of her life and herself.

It had been six weeks since she'd seen Billy. She was settled in school, and she'd quit having the dream. Later she would think of that moment and wonder why it couldn't have lasted all her life, why it just couldn't have gone on and on, with her in complete control of everything that mattered to her.

But of course it didn't, the way nothing can ever be good forever and nothing can ever be bad forever.

Because it was that same evening that she went to bed early, feeling so good about everything. She'd left her window open, the window that looked out on the courtyard, so the cool of the night could come into her room and make the heavy blanket of native wool, which she liked so much, feel comfortable.

She loved to sleep cold, loved it because it made her fresh and alive in the morning, but this particular time she would always wonder about leaving the window open—wonder what had made her do it.

Because with the window closed she might not have heard anything, might not have known what was going on. . . .

It was long after she'd gone to sleep, long after she was snuggled deep under the blanket and heavily into sleep that the persistent sound started.

It was a new sound, a strange sound, but a beautiful sound, and it cut through her sleep the way a warm knife moves through butter, until she was awake, only not really, and the sound was still there but still part of her sleep somehow, and even when she opened her eyes and looked up at the *vigas,* the sound continued.

Finally she recognized it as a kind of music, a muted flute sound, beautiful and lilting in the darkness of her room—almost sweet, the sound of the flute, sweet and soft and very much alive and rich.

She rubbed her eyes and thought she must be dreaming some new kind of very real dream. But then the door to her room opened and her mother came in wearing her housecoat, and in the moonlight in the room Janet could see the question in her eyes.

"What on earth . . . ?"

"I don't know."

Janet sat up. "It's coming from outside—outside the window."

Her mother moved to the window and looked out and then stood, stunned, staring outside.

"My God," she whispered. "It . . . it can't be."

"What?" Janet got out of bed, threw the blanket on the floor, and went to the window, and there she, too, stood frozen as she stared out into the courtyard. Only she couldn't say anything, couldn't form any words.

The moon was full, splashing blue-white across the courtyard so bright it would have been possible to read. It was an almost unreal light, beautiful and as strange as the moonlight in her dream, different because it was alive and real, but somehow the same, too, and the music from the flute was almost something you could see, like a part of the moonlight, like a part of the night, like a part of everything Janet was and ever would be.

In the middle of the courtyard, washed in the moonlight as though dipped in some wonderful silvery liquid, stood Billy Honcho.

He was playing a flute, which he held with a kind of elemental grace, and if the truth were known, it took Janet a full minute to recognize him.

Because the figure who stood in the moonlight in the courtyard was not the Billy Honcho Janet knew; the man who stood tall and graceful sending out music meant for her soul was not some old drunk.

He was a warrior, dressed in buckskins bleached white and made whiter by the moon and covered with such intricate beadwork that it looked painted on the leather, with a chest shield of quills and beads in the shape of an eagle with wings outstretched, and all down the length of each sleeve was a ribbon of quills and more beads.

His braids were clean and braided with leather strapping worked into the hair and bits of ermine fluff at the ends, and on his back in a case was a short bow and a few arrows, and he was more than beautiful, more than stunning.

He was something from the past, something real and alive from the past of all men. And as they watched, the flute music ended and the flute came down, and he disappeared like a part of the moonlight. Janet's mother swore softly, like a prayer, and Janet choked up and felt like crying and soon did, with great tears moving down her cheeks, and she didn't even feel them.

She wanted to call but no sound came, only the tears.

**10**

**"He's courting you, and you'll have** to put a stop to it. It's as simple as that."

It was the next morning, and they'd been up most of the night, sitting and talking, and now Janet's mother sipped coffee—from the fourth pot—and talked to Janet at the wooden kitchen table.

Janet stared down at the table. There were some crumbs near the edge, and she carefully scooped them up and put them in the trash and sat down again.

"You're wrong, Mother." She shrugged. "And even if you're right, what's the difference? Where's the harm?"

"He's an old man, and you're ... you're ..."

"A young white girl. That's what you want to say, isn't it?"

"Janet, that wasn't fair...."

Janet softened. "I'm sorry. I know you don't mean that—it's just that I think you're wrong. He's just trying to make up with me for—for drinking, for all of it."

"No. He's courting you. I've read several books on Indians, did it when we decided to move out here. Like I said, the flute and the finery definitely mean courting. It's an old ritual, the way braves have always courted maidens." Her eyes washed, and she smiled, remembering. "It *was* beautiful, wasn't it? But still, you've got to put a stop to it. Right away."

Janet shook her head. "There's nothing to stop, Mother. You're wrong—he isn't courting me. He's just . . ." She ran out of words. "It's just something true and wonderful he's doing, and I think it would hurt him to make him stop."

"If you don't, it will just be worse later. You'll see." She suddenly shook her head. "Lord, listen to me, sounding like an ordinary mother. But it's the truth. Stop it now, or you'll have trouble later."

And it ended there, not with anger, because they had grown too close for anger. It ended because they had been up all night and were tired and needed some sleep and because they had both had their say and knew the other's position.

They went to bed, though it was day, and slept until late afternoon. When they awakened—almost at the same time—it was becoming dusk, and it was going to be another clear fall night. They ate supper or breakfast, depending on how they wished to call it, and there was a kind of quiet peace between them.

"You missed school today." Janet's mother helped clear the table before going into her studio to work. "I'll give you a note for tomorrow."

"Tomorrow is Saturday—there's no school. I'll take a note Monday."

And they moved into the night, neither talking of the night before but both wondering if Billy would come again.

They did not have long to wait. This night the moon was still full, and just after ten, when they normally would have been going to bed but were now still awake because they'd slept all day, just after the moon had completely risen, Janet was moving through the kitchen where she was baking bread when she heard a solid *thump* sound somewhere outside.

It was the sound a brick might make when thrown down into dirt, and it seemed to be coming from the courtyard.

She went to the door and pulled it open, but for a second she couldn't see anything. Then, over by the wall in the half shadow, she again heard the thump, and as she watched, a pony moved out of the shadow into the moonlight, and she caught her breath.

It was a small pinto pony, compact and covered with black-and-white splotches where the hair changed color—the classic "Indian" pony.

All over it were painted different signs, some that looked like targets, others that seemed to be large handprints, and still other signs that appeared to be large bird wings. Around one eye was painted a circle, and a braided rope went from the pony's jaw back to his neck.

On his back was a striped, woven riding blanket, and as she watched, he stamped his forefeet into the dirt—causing the *thump* sound.

Bits of steam came from his nostrils, delicate little puffs in the moonlight, and he snorted when Janet moved suddenly to take her hand off the door handle because it was getting cold.

After a moment she looked around the rest of the courtyard but could see nothing. Billy was gone, had come and left the pony and was gone into the night, and she was turning to talk to her mother, who had come up behind her and let out a startled breath: just as Janet was turning, Billy jumped over the low courtyard wall on a beautiful white horse larger than the pony.

The horse jumped silently, kicking bits of dirt up when it struck, and wheeled in one fluid motion when it landed so that it stood sideways to Janet and her mother, stood side-on with its sides heaving but still without sound.

It had all happened in less than two seconds, the jump and the wheel and the horse standing, and on top of him Billy, a part of the horse, dressed in the same white buckskins he'd worn the night before, cloaked in the same white beauty. He looked down on them in haughty silence.

The pony stamped, and it was the only sound. Neither Janet nor her mother could even breathe; they could not or would not do anything to break the spell that Billy and the two horses cast on the night. Finally, with the two women staring almost openmouthed, Billy produced the flute from some recess in his buckskins and began to play.

It was not the same haunting melody of the previous night, but a more lively song that was slightly quicker and seemed to roll out of the flute and into the night almost with humor, or with a feeling lighter than air.

At first there was only the music, and if that had been all that happened, it would have been enough. But before the melody was four seconds old, Janet's mother nudged her from behind and whispered in her ear.

"The horse. Look at the horse!"

Janet let out her breath, realizing now that she'd been holding it all this time, and did as she was told—she studied the horse.

At first it was too subtle to be really noticeable, but after a moment she could see that the horse's front shoulders were rolling, moving in time to the music, and then his feet followed the movement of his shoulders and lifted from the ground in slight patting motions, and it was clear that the horse was dancing. Not just doing tricks, or moving to some hidden command, but moving *with* the music, so that soon Billy and the horse were rolling from side to side and around in a half circle as a part of the music from the flute and a part of the night and the moonlight, all mixed together, so that Janet, without knowing she was doing it, reached out with one hand to touch it, feel it, be a part of it. . . .

It was exquisite. A moment, a piece of time so rare and wonderful that she wanted to freeze it, make it last forever, keep it.

The horse waltzed around with the same rolling motion until the music was finished and the flute vanished back into some hidden place in the buckskins, and then Billy sat straight on his horse and looked directly at Janet and then to the pony and back to Janet. His meaning was unmistakable.

He wanted Janet to come riding with him on the pony, and she moved forward, could no more have refused him than she could have stopped breathing, and for the same reasons, but before she could take a step, her mother stepped in front of her.

"No!" And for that second her mother was more than just a woman, was some kind of wild creature protecting its young, and Janet turned in surprise at the sound of her voice, the savagery of it.

"No! She will not go with you—there is—there is too much right now. For her. She's too young."

But she became confused—angry but confused —and Billy rode forward on the white horse, glided across the ground like white fog, so that he was sitting over her, and Janet could see the nostrils of the horse right next to her mother's head, and they were pushing out rolls of steam like smoke, like dream smoke.

"No . . ." Janet's mother tried again, but her voice wavered, and then a strange thing happened because something passed between Billy and her mother that could almost be seen.

He said nothing, made no change in his expression as he sat there on the white horse, but something came from his eyes and moved down to Janet's mother.

"But . . ."

Her mother fought the thing for a moment, battled with something inside herself that Janet couldn't understand, and then seemed to sag a little back against the door.

"I'm sorry—I thought all the wrong things, from before, when I was with a man. Her father. I should have known better, that it wasn't always wrong or that—you will not hurt her." And here the iron came back in her voice. "Not in any way, do you understand?"

Still he said nothing, but only looked down, and yet there was that thing, that strange feeling or look or smell or mind-touch that passed between them, and when it was done, they knew each other in a way that few people ever know each other, and Janet felt that she'd seen something almost miraculous. Then her mother turned and her voice was a whisper, a soft *whush* of words.

"You can go if you want to." She smiled. "He won't . . . won't hurt you. I was wrong about him."

And Janet moved to the pony and threw herself onto its back and sat up and picked up the braided hand loop in the pony's mane, which she took firmly in her hand. And Billy moved through the gate instead of jumping the wall, and the pony followed out into the dark of the road, the still wash of the night and moonlight. Billy headed off in the direction of the mountains and the pony followed, with Janet on its back, and never once did she hesitate.

# 11

**They moved through the night like a** soft knife through water, so that the night opened in front of them and closed behind and left them just in their small pocket of moonlight and silence. Later, when Janet tried to remember the ride, all she could honestly remember was that her mind was blank and that images of great beauty would cycle through, come and go, but not really stay so that she could lock them in her thoughts.

They were out of town very soon, away from all buildings, and past the gate to the pueblo, on out into the country, up into the foothills that led to the mountains.

Riding was easy. She was amazed that it was so simple. She'd ridden some in the past, when she was a small girl, but then only in circles on led small ponies.

This was, if anything, easier; the pony moved to keep its weight directly under her, kept her comfortable and balanced, and soon she relaxed her grip on the braid and began to move with the motion of the horse, which made it easier still, and once she relaxed, she began to see things in the night.

Once a small nighthawk swooped past, not four inches from her face, out of the night and back into it in silence, and she actually felt the kiss of wind from his wing, a brush so light on her cheek that it might have been imagined, a kiss by a ghost.

Billy moved ahead of her as they got out of the buildings and left the road and moved across the flats of scrub and piñon, and she watched him and felt ... felt close and strange and safe and wonderful in a way she couldn't understand and didn't pick at because she sensed that to pick at it would ruin it.

It wasn't love, not really, but something very much like it, and there was awe in it and richness and quietness and softness and power, and the feelings all cycled through the way the images did, so that she couldn't remember later any single one, couldn't say to herself *I felt this way* at any given time. It was very much like the touch of wind from the wing of the nighthawk, the way the feelings moved through her mind as they rode—soft touches of thoughts that didn't always tie together but were always good and left her mind with a good taste.

She wasn't cold, and that, too, surprised her. It was a chilly night, though very still, yet she wasn't cold even with the movement of the horse, and she supposed it was because she was so caught up in everything else.

The trip across the high desert, out of town, and up through the scrub and sand washes might have taken two hours or two days, she didn't know, had no way of knowing or caring; but before dawn they were in the pine forests of the foothills and moving through the rich smells of the pine needles around them.

The moon went down while they were in the pines, but enough light came from where it went over the horizon to light their way, and Billy moved ahead of her over a series of ridges, rolling high mountain meadows, through the dark, and finally down a last, sloping incline to some more trees and through the trees and down a shallow bank to the edge of a pool of water.

It was not the same pool as the small pond in her dream. This one was much larger, but she gasped when she saw it because it was so peaceful; around the edges, out about ten feet, there was a thin layer of ice, and the water beyond was so still it was practically impossible to see where the ice ended and the water began.

Billy stopped his horse on the grass near the pond and dismounted and signaled for Janet to do the same, and he took both horses off into the trees and tied them.

Then he came back, and he was holding the striped blanket from the pony, which he unfolded and spread on the ground, and still in silence and all with hand motions he told her to sit on the blanket and make herself comfortable. When she'd done so, he moved off to the edge of the pond and spread his arms and sang a song, or recited some poetry, in Indian, standing tall with the white buckskins and the night around him, and although Janet couldn't understand any of the words in the song, she recognized it as a form of praying from the tone in his voice and the way he stood.

When he'd finished singing, the first sound he'd made all night, he squatted with his back to Janet, still facing the pond, and sat in silence for what seemed like hours.

Now Janet became cold, and she wrapped the blanket around her shoulders—he didn't turn when she moved—and hunched warmth into her shoulders and began to feel strange. It was the strange feeling that comes of not having slept, the messy-dream feeling and burned-out sensation that takes over the mind when sleep is needed, and she wondered if she should tell Billy and was going to say something—perhaps that she would like a little sleep—when he stood up and turned and faced her.

For a time he stared down on her, sitting huddled in the blanket, and while he stood this way, the sun came up in back of him—or at least lightened the sky and silhouetted him with a faint red glow—and she could make out the features of his face better than in the dark, and she could see that they were soft and gentle.

"Why do you do this?" he asked, and his voice had a hoarse quality that was somehow close. "I am an old man, and yet you followed me up into the hills—why do you do this?"

But he didn't want an answer, not really, and she sat quietly watching him, waiting, and she wanted to touch him but knew that it would be wrong, so she just sat, but of all the things she didn't question, she didn't ask herself what she was doing in the mountain with Billy.

That had come up, once, during the ride. A brief question, a touch of inquisitiveness, a smell of wonder; but it had vanished immediately, because even not knowing what was going to happen, she knew she couldn't miss it.

That it had all been strange, almost weird, she knew and understood—but that it could have been stopped or changed, that she could have not come with him or not be involved with him was utterly impossible. It was all natural, like rain, like wind. . . .

"And it is this way and so," Billy interrupted her thinking. "When there was no time, back even before there was no time and no coyote to think of things, the Great Mother sent two crows, and they flew and flew until their wings were tired, looking for a place to land, a place to *be*."

He paused, still standing over her, and she looked up and nodded, though she wasn't sure why she was nodding. She was following the story, but had no idea where it was going or what it truly meant, or why he was telling it to her.

"When at last their wings could no longer support them, when they had flown through darkness and it seemed they would have to fly thus forever, they fell to earth.

"Down and down they fell, end over end, two black birds tumbling through the blackness of before time, and when finally they hit the earth, it was at the same place at which they had started to fly, the same place they'd been put by the Great Mother.

"And it is this way and so. Where they landed was this place we now stand, as it always will be the place where The People stand. Because where we start is where we end and where we end is where we start, and that is the end of the story."

He nodded and sat, or dropped into a squat, facing her.

"I ..." She didn't know what to say, what was expected of her. "It is a good story. ..." She let it fall off, waiting.

"It is the ritual story always told in courtship between a young brave and the maiden who rode his pony."

"Oh."

The light was brighter now, a yellow-red glow over everything, and she looked around at the trees and down at the pond without trying to look around at the trees or down at the pond.

"Now they ride in trucks, and there is no ritual." His voice was tight with scorn. "They ride in trucks and do not mind the beauty of things, the way they used to do.

"Now we would sit for a day and another night, and I would go and kill a deer, and you would eat of it, and when we went down the mountain, we would be married."

She said nothing, but she thought of the deer that he mentioned and that brought back the dream, and she wondered if she could have read somewhere about the deer and marriage business. It seemed to fit so well.

"Now they ride in pickups and go to the church with the walls and the man in black with the backward collar says they are married, and so they are married, and then they drive around with much sound on the horns of the trucks and get drunk on beer so their heads are loose and go to bed and that is that . . . tscha!" He turned and spat. "That is less than nothing. Where is the beauty in that?"

He stood, an upward movement that seemed to lift him, and spread his arms to show his buckskins. "Look. Oh, look, I stand in good relation to the gods. Is not this suit worthy?"

She looked up, smiled. In the full light the beadwork was incredibly fine—almost beyond human doing.

"My mother made this suit. I was married to Easter in it." He smiled, and his ugly teeth did not show but only beauty. "Isn't this better than a pickup and horns making sounds?"

She nodded. And meant it.

"Ahh, and it was this way and so. Back before time men were men, and there were no horns and no trucks. And no wine." A sadness crept in. "No wine—only beauty."

"Tell me." She sat up, wrapped the blanket tighter. "Tell me what it was like . . . all of it."

He looked at her, let his eyes close and open. "You would not believe it."

"Tell me anyway. Please."

And he stood, and began moving and talking, and in less than a second Janet was whisked back before time.

**12**

**It was more than the way he talked,** the words rolling like half-music from his tongue, rolling down and surrounding her with what they said and were; and it was more than what they said and were; and it was more than the way he moved, sometimes with immense grace, half-dancing, and sometimes with jerky movements, but still dancing, only not just dancing but *telling.*

It was everything, all of it came together— the movement and the words—and Janet thought this must be the way it was back when people lived in caves and the hunters returned from the hunt and told the story of how it went around the fire.

Something moved inside her, watching him talk-move, and it was a strange and new and yet somehow very, very old thing, and it scared her but left her feeling more alive than she'd ever felt.

"We had wars," he started. "And it was thus and so that after the Great Mother gave us this place and this mountain as our own, there were others who came from the south, way down where they had nothing but sand and dryness because they had displeased the Great Mother and that is all she would give them."

And here even his body showed the scorn, the utter degradation of the others who came from the south and who had displeased the Great Mother, and Janet felt almost ill at the thought of them.

"And they came up north to take what was ours, because we had water and good soil and stood in good relation to the gods. Tscha! They were fools and thought they were warriors of such stature that they brought their women and children and even their dogs with little skids to carry their meager supplies and clothing."

His movements dipped and whirled so that Janet could see the dogs and children and the little skids, poles going back alongside the dogs and the dust of their walking, and she squinted, looking out with her mind at the picture of them walking and coming.

"We met them in the big flats of desert out away from our corn so they could not ruin crops, because we did not know if they understood the saving of crops even in battle. And we heard later that they had told their women to be ready to live in the small rooms of the pueblo by nightfall."

He minced to show the women laughing and dancing, and Janet caught herself smiling as she saw them—women from an age dead and gone centuries before she was born—getting ready to move into the pueblo.

"Ahh, there was fighting that day that the people from the south could not expect, could not believe. They came to kill, to conquer, and instead they died, and their women sang the death songs for many, many days.

"We took our women with us to the battlefield to show them the scorn we held for them, to show them how little they were. And we stood in ranks with lines straight, and the woman in back, and we used the big clubs with the sharp points on the end, and we killed them as they came at us, killed them and threw them over our shoulders like meat for dogs, and the women in back stuck little knives in the backs of their heads to make sure they were dead and cut them to show what we thought of them as men, and when that day was done, the people from the south were no more, no more, and the crows were fat for a whole summer with what they had to eat.

"We threw their bodies down in the gully south of the pueblo and took their women and children into our tribe, and those people were no more, nothing but a stink in the afternoon."

He stopped suddenly, and Janet could smell the blood and dust in the heat of that day, could hear the women screaming and wailing, could see the wild savagery of the battle, and a part of her was sickened by it and made sad by the women's crying and the children without fathers because they'd been killed in the battle.

But another part was thrilled, was excited by the story of the battle, and she related to the winning side because she sat now with one of the warriors. And as she looked up, his age vanished and the time vanished so that what stood before her was not Billy Honcho, old man in buckskins, but a young brave.

Tall, he stood, shining with his leather clothes in the new morning light, fresh from a battle three hundred years old, fresh with ancient blood and victory and with strength and sureness showing in and around him like something alive, a glow of life, and she reached out from where she sat, let the blanket fall and reached out.

And Billy reached down and took her hand and held it for a second and released it, and there was much that went between them, whole *worlds* that went between them when they touched there in that cold, still morning on the edge of the partially frozen pond.

She loved him. Not so much him, and it was not so much gushy love, but she loved what he was when he told the story, loved not just what he was but what he should have been, loved what he *could* have been if the time had been right for him.

She loved him. Because he was the Indian in the dream, but he was more than that too; more than simply a dream person, because when he'd told the story of the battle, she had actually seen him change and become a warrior in the fight. And even now, after the story and battle were done and he stood silent, he was still all that he should and could have been, and she loved him for that; and all the wine and all that other part of his life were gone—shed like old skin or waste. Gone.

And what was left she loved and more, it was more than just love—she was awed by the strength of him, the power that had taken him and made his nostrils flare and his eyes blow fire and youth, and it scared her a little. But only a little, and it was a good fear—almost a fear of herself and the kind of fear that kept her out of trouble.

They were silent the rest of the morning, silent as the sun came up and made them warm, and they sat, Billy down by the pond, Janet on the blanket, through the whole day, off and on dozing and getting warm, and in the middle of the afternoon Billy uncoiled and stood and turned, and his face was soft, but still young.

"It is time."

She had been dreamily looking at his back and the pond, staring into her mind, and she stood with him. "Time for what?"

"You must take the pony and go back down the mountain. I will stay."

*No,* she thought, but it didn't come out, didn't make it to her mouth. *No* cut through her thoughts and seared across the middle of her brain; *no this is wrong no don't do this no you don't have to stay on the mountain, no I love you no don't stay because there is no need; no, no, no. . . .*

"You do not move." His tone admonished. "You have something to say?"

"I would rather you didn't do this—didn't stay." Some part of her wanted to run to him, run screaming and hold him and cry, but some new part wouldn't let her do it, made her reserved. She hated the new part, but understood it.

"It is time." He repeated, his voice flat. "I have done most things once. It is no good to do things twice. Down there," he pointed with his face back in the direction of the pueblo, "there is only the wine. Only that."

"But . . ."

"It is time."

"I . . ."

"I know. I feel the same." And a kind of torment slid into his words, a tremor, a smell of something unsure. "Do you think this thing is easy? Do not make it harder for me. It is time. Go. Now."

She turned and walked back into the trees where he had tied the horses and untied the pony and climbed onto its back and rode out into the meadow and down in the direction of the pueblo and town because she knew it was something she had to do, had to leave him now, though it tore at her to do it.

She rode out across the meadow and started down the trail that led back to town and home, a fifteen-year-old girl with a mother who was divorced and with Julio who followed her and made the sounds in his throat so she would turn and see him ignoring her. But at the last moment, just as the pony started on the down trail, she turned to look at Billy once more because she knew she would never see him again, and she loved him.

She loved him. For what he could have been, and she knew that he loved her the same way, for what they could have been. But when she turned to look, he had his back to her and was facing the pond and his shoulders were straight, and she knew he was waiting, waiting for his last battle, and that he wouldn't be thinking about her. And she turned and rode down the mountain, and she did not look back again, did not once look back, though she cried and cried and was still crying so badly in grief for a love that was gone before it came, still crying so deeply and tearingly that when she rode into the courtyard of her home, she could not stop, could not get off the pony, and had to get help from her mother, who came out and half-carried, half-led her into the house and only patted her on the forehead and did not ask the reason for the crying.

After a time she slept, but it was not the kind of sleep that helps except temporarily, and she knew, even as she went to sleep, that she would probably spend the rest of her life trying not to think about Billy Honcho, which was something she wanted but did not want at the same time; and when she awakened in the night, because she was sinking, just sinking forever all the way down, when she jerked awake she thought first of Billy, and she forced sleep to come again quickly because even the dream, which she knew was coming, even the dream was better than being awake.

# Epilogue

**It was the same dream, exactly.**

The doe was white, and she dipped her muzzle to drink out of the milk-shimmering white of the pool, which shattered moonlight when her nose rippled the surface of the still water.

Drops of silver liquid spilled from her mouth when she raised her head from drinking, and it was all so beautiful and stark and white and still that Janet thought, Oh.

Just oh. And she reached out a hand in the dream to touch the deer, the way she might touch an especially soft and beautiful flower or a piece of delicate lace.

Then the brave appeared.

With the threat that somehow wasn't a threat, he moved out of the brush and nocked an arrow to his bow and raised the bow and drew the arrow and looked down the shaft, aiming, so that light came from his eyes and moved down the shaft of the arrow out across the pond to the neck of the deer. He was beautiful, too, though in a different way from the deer.

And even as she watched, he released the arrow, and it flew out of the bow down the light from his eyes and out across the still, white beauty of the pond. Like a white line in the moonlight it flew, making and leaving a line of cold fire; it streaked out of the bow and across the pond, and she could see it moving, almost slowly, but with infinite power and deadly intent from the bow and across the pond, leaving no shadow and no sound until it buried itself in the neck of the doe with a soft *thwup* sound.

The doe arched her neck and back up and over in an agonized torque, a fierce arc of pain and lost life, and she turned to her side and went down gently, the way a ballerina might sink in a death scene, and it was all done quietly so that even the light wasn't disturbed. And when she was dead and down in the dream, bent and gone the way all things dead are bent and gone, Janet turned in the dream to look at the Indian and accuse him of this ugly thing, blame him; but when she turned, the Indian was gone. Or perhaps he had never been there and was all part of a dream within a dream.

Because in the dream when she turned to see the fallen doe again, it was also gone, or perhaps had never been there; she couldn't tell.

All that remained was the still white of the pool of water, which was part of the moonlight and part of the dream, and soon that, too, was gone, and there was nothing but sleep....

Gary Paulsen is the author of
many critically acclaimed books for young people,
including three Newbery Honor Books,
*The Winter Room, Hatchet,* and *Dogsong.*
His newest book for Delacorte Press is *Canyons.*
Gary Paulsen lives with his wife and son
in northern Minnesota.